March Has
Horse's Ears
and Other Stories

March Has Horse's Ears
and Other Stories

BY ROBERT NYE

Illustrated by Dorothy Maas

HILL AND WANG : *New York*

AcM

Manufactured in the United States of America

by American Book–Stratford Press, Inc.

1234567890

for
Jack,
Taliesin
&
Malory

Contents

March Has
Horse's Ears
and Other Stories

❧ March Has Horse's Ears ❧

There was once a prince called March who had everything a prince could want: white horses, high-flying hawks, faithful hounds, his own private bank full of gold and silver, and a bathroom next door to his bedroom. Everyone said, "What a lucky man! How happy he must be!" But March was not happy. He had a secret. Day and night he worried lest someone should find it out, so terrible it was to him. And the secret was this: March had horse's ears!

The only person in the land who knew the secret was the royal barber, and he had been forced to swear a solemn oath that he would never tell anyone. "If you so much as breathe a word about a certain unmentionable subject," said March, adjusting the flaps on the special helmet he wore to hide his deformity, "if you even dare whisper it to a little bird—off comes your head!"

The barber was a lean, sad man, like a pair of rusty scissors. After he found out about his master's ears he grew even leaner and sadder and rustier. March himself seldom smiled, but the barber *never* smiled—because, after all, if the secret were ever revealed his fate would be worse than the prince's. Ridicule is bad enough, but beheading is certainly worse.

The secret began to make the barber quite ill. He had dreadful dreams in which he saw and heard himself shouting to the Society for the Protection of Royal Barbers: "March has horse's ears! March has horse's ears!" And the audience clapped and stamped and laughed. "Hurrah! Ha! Ha! March has horse's ears!" And then, in his dream, he saw the block and the executioner, old Scroop, with his keen-edged axe, and. . . .

He always woke up screaming, in a cold sweat.

At last, the barber went to the royal doctor. The doctor was no fool. After tapping the barber's chest and peering at his tongue and making him say "Aaaaaah" and "Ninety-nine," he said, "There's nothing wrong with you physically, at all. I think something is preying upon your mind. You have a secret—something you are afraid to talk about. That's what's making you ill, isn't it?"

The barber was so frightened he almost fell out of his chair.

He wondered if the doctor could have overheard his heart muttering, "March-has-horse's-ears! March-has-horse's-ears!" He pressed his lips tightly together, terrified that the secret might come jumping out.

The doctor shrugged. "If you don't tell someone this thing that's bothering you I wouldn't like to say what might happen."

"And if I *do* tell someone," cried the poor barber, "I lose my head. What a situation! If I've got to die, I'd sooner die with my head on."

The doctor twiddled his thumbs and thought about this for a while. Then he said, "Look here, why don't you just go and tell your precious secret to the ground? That way you'd be rid of it. And surely you wouldn't lose your head for telling the ground?"

The barber considered this an excellent solution. He ran all day until he came to the river that marked the boundary of March's lands. Then he lay down with his cheek against the riverbank and whispered the dreadful words, "March has horse's ears! March has horse's ears!" Immediately, he felt better. His colour and

appetite came back on the long walk home. He even regained enough of his old gusto to cut patterns in the air with the scissors—snip, snop, snap—when he was trimming the prince's hair.

Now, on the spot where the barber had told his secret to the ground a thick crop of reeds sprang up. One day, many months later, March got married, and he prepared a public feast to celebrate the marriage, sending out an invitation to the finest piper in the world to come and make music to entertain his guests. On the way to March's castle the piper passed by the place where the reeds were growing and, as his old pipe was much the worse for wear, he cut a reed and fashioned a new pipe from it.

When the guests had eaten and drunk to their bellies' content, March called in the piper and commanded him to play.

The piper bowed low. He placed the pipe to his lips. He blew. And the pipe said, "March has horse's ears! March has horse's ears!"

The guests began to giggle behind their hands, then to laugh openly. March snatched up his sword and seized the piper by the throat.

"Please, Your Eternity," spluttered the poor musician, "have mercy on me! It's not my fault. I tried to play the music that has melted hearts the world over. But the pipe is bewitched! Try it for yourself!"

March glared at him for a moment in angry disbelief. Then he threw down his sword and took the pipe in his hands. He blew. "March has horse's ears," said the pipe.

The hall was in an uproar. Everyone was laughing. Some were rolling about on the floor, kicking their legs in the air. But a

sudden silence fell as March's bride, the Princess Probability, rose to her feet and went to her husband's side where he stood, blushing and dismayed, staring at the pipe.

"How many gentlemen present have horse's ears?" she asked the company. "Only one. My March. It is a sign of his difference from you, for he is your prince. Besides," she turned to her husband with a smile, "I *like* horse's ears. They will no doubt stand up intelligently when I call you. Now take off that ridiculous helmet!"

And she kissed him—first on one ear, then on the other.

After this, everyone agreed that horse's ears were just the thing to have. The more foppish lords of the court even adopted the fashion of wearing false ones. As for March, he forgave the piper and the pipe and never made any further effort to hide his ears. As for the barber, he grew fat and jolly, and talked and talked and talked—thus setting another fashion, which barbers have followed to this day.

∼§ Cooked for Fifteen §∼

I

Some people have mice and some people have spiders, but Farmer Dewy and his wife had fairies. They were overrun with them. They had fairies upstairs, faries downstairs, fairies in the kitchen, fairies in the cowhouse, fairies under the bed chattering and plotting and playing flutes all night long, fairies up in the attic stamping and counter-marching and playing football in hobnail boots, fairies sniggering, fairies blubbering, fairies on the top of the Welsh dresser, and fairies—of course—at the bottom of the garden.

When, one Sunday dinner-time, his wife carried in the big dish

: 9

with the chicken on it, and Farmer Dewy lifted the dish-cover to
find two fairies sitting among the ruins, pulling the wishbone, he
decided things had gone far enough. In fact, rather too far.

"It's all your fault," he moaned at his wife. "If you hadn't gone
offering that fairy lady your old blue gown——"

"How was I to know she'd be offended?" demanded Mrs.
Dewy. "It's not everyone can be so choosey. Do you think it was
because it was old or because it was blue? Bessie Dunlop says fairy
ladies will only wear green. But then there's others say they've
seen them jump over the moon in blue petticoats; so perhaps it

was just too big? Regular little fashion-madam! Tore it in shreds, she did. Furious, she was. Oh dear! what's that?"

It was more fairies shaking a white pepper of dust down through the cracks in the ceiling and into her rice-pudding.

"Clear off!" bellowed Farmer Dewy, banging on the beams with his spoon. "Can't you leave us alone? The wife meant well enough, d'you hear? There's no call for you to keep on plaguing us out of our wits. Besides," he added, softly, in case they heard him, "I don't really believe in you."

"I have a green dress," wailed his wife, "a new one, with a red velvet bow and how to wash it on a little shiny label. You can take it to your cousin, or Queen, or whatever she is, and welcome. Only, please, leave us be!"

The answer was a fearful grinding and crunching. Both Dewys ran upstairs to find the fairies had made a neat job of sawing their bed in two. "It's criminal!" cried Mrs. Dewy, throwing her apron over her head.

That night all was quiet. The Dewys woke up after their first good sleep for weeks, without any buckets being emptied in their faces or feathers applied to their toes. They crept downstairs, hardly able to believe their luck. . . .

And a good job they couldn't—because Mrs. Dewy discovered her best Swansea china stuffed in the coal-scuttle, and Farmer Dewy went out to find the cows milked dry and the horses in a muck-sweat, having been ridden until their wind was broken.

Farmer Dewy consulted a cunning man, a wizard. "Just because the wife took pity on a little fairy lady with no clothes in the rain," he explained, "and the ungrateful thing got in a huff about the colour or something. You know what women are."

"Yes, indeed. Well, I'm glad you came to me," said the wizard, rubbing his long cucumber of a nose. "I have just the, um, plan for you to get rid of your unwanted, er, guests. Yes, indeed. You know that these what-d'you-call-'ems, thingummybobs——"

"Fairies?" suggested Farmer Dewy.

"Exactly. Well, you know that when someone moves from one what's-it to another, house that is, they leave the what's-it?"

"But I'm not giving up my farm just——"

"No, no, indeed. But you must, eh, pretend, dissemble, dissimulate, hoodwink, and all that. When they think you've, you know, aah, gone, then they'll, you know, aah——"

"Yes?" cried Farmer Dewy.

"Yes, indeed!"

Well, the Dewys packed up all their furniture and belongings and banged about the farmhouse telling each other (and, of course, as they hoped, the fairies) that they were off to a new life in a new house over the hill in another village. Then they set off down the road with their wagon, as noisily and busily as they could.

They had not gone far when they met their old friend the blacksmith, out for a stroll with his dog. He was surprised to see them perched up on top of their furniture, lumbering out of the village. "Leaving us is it then, Dewy?"

Before either Dewy had a chance to reply, the lid of the upright piano was lifted from inside and a little lark-voice cried: "Yes, that's right, Bellows-Face. We're all going to live in a new house over the hill. Halloo! Hey! Hurrah!"

"So much for that gizzard of a wizard!" moaned Mrs. Dewy, as

they turned sadly for home again. "I told you not to trust the old what's-it with all his what's-its. You must go to the wise woman, the witch!"

So Farmer Dewy went to the witch. And the witch listened carefully to his long story and then she said, "Can your wife catch a sparrow?" and when Farmer Dewy said, rather doubtfully, suspecting a joke, that yes, she *could* catch a sparrow, the witch looked over her shoulder, spat in her cauldron, put on her spectacles, and began whispering in his ear, telling him what he must do. . . .

2

At breakfast next morning Mrs. Dewy laid down her knife and fork (which were not much use anyway as the fairies had filled the sausages with sawdust), cleared her thoat, winked at her husband, and said: "How many men did you say you were having over today to help cut the corn in the big field, dear?"

"Fifteen," said Farmer Dewy.

"I beg your pardon?"

"FIFTEEN! And they'll all be coming up here for a bite of supper. See to it that there's a good meal ready for them, won't you?"

"They'll have no cause to complain," said his wife. "We'll feed them according to our means."

Late that afternoon, long after her husband had gone off to direct work in the cornfield, Mrs. Dewy went out into the yard and caught a sparrow. She feathered it, trussed it, and roasted it in the oven. Then she poured a few grains of salt in a hazel-nut shell, filled a thimble with mashed potato, and set sparrow, salt and thimble, with half a slice of stale bread, on the table.

"There!" she said loudly. "I only hope that'll satisfy them. It's the best I can do, anyway."

And she went out into the fields to call the men home to supper.

No sooner was she gone than all the fairies in the house gathered round the table, gazing at the meal in dismay.

"I've lived a longish while," said one, "in fact, I was born just after the earth herself; but I've never seen a sight like *that!*"

"Nor me," agreed another. "Let's leave these poor people alone. We've ruined them."

The others nodded. "Who before this was ever so hard up as to serve just one shrimpy sparrow as a supper for fifteen hungry men?"

And the fairies left then and there and never troubled Farmer Dewy and his wife again. Only the sparrow did *not* live happily ever after, but then it's not every sparrow that has the honour of being cooked for fifteen.

❧ Half a Yard ❧

Old Peg was tired of lending things to the fairies. Not a day would pass without a knock at her door or a tap at her window or even, most ominous of all, a scrabbling in her chimney—and there would be a little man with a turkey feather in his cap or a tiny woman in a green gown standing on the doorstep, or on the other side of the pane peering in, or even—covered in soot—sitting on her nice clean hearth, and asking if they might borrow this, that, or the other. Old Peg had to admit that the fairies knew their manners, and were always polite and gentle; but, all the same, they *were* a bit of a nuisance, especially those who insisted on using her chimney as a public thoroughfare.

Matters came to a head one night when Old Peg had gone to bed early and was almost asleep. All at once she heard a noise on the windowpane: knock, knock, knock; Knock, *knock*, KNOCK. At first she ignored it, thinking it was only the long arm of the apple tree, heavy with apples, that stood beside her cottage. "It's only the branch," she told herself, sleepily, "only the old branch in the wind knocking its knuckles against the pane."

But the noise went on and on: knock, knock, knock; Knock, *knock*, KNOCK; and it grew more insistent and impatient. And then she heard a sharp voice crying, "Old Peg! Old Peg! It's not the apple branch—it's me, Eyelash Jones. Let me in!"

Muttering, Old Peg slid out of bed and threw the window open, nearly dislodging the little man who was dangling by one hand outside and had been tapping on the glass with the other.

"Well, well, well, what do you want at this time of night?" she demanded angrily. "It's a poor thing when a body can't even take the sleep due to her, for fairies banging and skittering at her window fit to wake the dead."

The little fellow grinned cheekily. "Not so much of your complaining, Old Peg," he said. "Don't we always pay you for what you lend us?"

Now if it had not been so late and she had not been in a bad temper, Old Peg would probably have admitted the truth of this. The fairies did always reward her well for the things she was kind enough to lend them: every morning she would find a bright sixpence, or a crisp warm loaf neatly wrapped in a dock-leaf, waiting for her on the doorstep. But she was in no mood to remember such things.

"What is it you want, you daft little fly-by-night?" she said, irritably.

"Well," began Eyelash Jones, bobbing up and down from the bough and waggling his ears in excitement, "I was going to eat an apple, you see. A lovely, red-coated, crisp outside and juicy inside one, all full of summer and——"

"Gracious goodness!" cried Old Peg. "I know what my own apples are like, you great minnow of nothing! Come to the point!"

"This is the point," said Eyelash Jones. And he opened his mouth wide in a toothless grin. "You see? I have no teeth. And I was wondering if—you can't be using them at this time of night, in fact I've seen you putting them to bed in a tumbler, otherwise of course I wouldn't presume to ask—but I was wondering if—as a magnanimous and absolutely immortal personal favour—I wouldn't need them *all*, even, just a few—and just so as I can really appreciate that marvellous tasty apple—well, to cut a frothy story short: *Can I borrow your false teeth?*"

Old Peg almost fell out of the bedroom window in her rage.

"Go away!" she shouted. "Go and jump off a toadstool! Borrow my false teeth, indeed! The sauce! The cheek of it!"

And she slammed the window shut with such a bang that the little man was knocked from the apple branch and fell, head-first, in the water-butt.

"Can I borrow your false teeth?" Old Peg mimicked the little man's voice as she got back into bed and pulled the covers up over her head. "Well I'm blowed!"

She soon forgot the fairy, and fell asleep worrying about more important matters: the huge tree-trunk she had in her garden that needed chopping, to lay in logs against the winter days coming; and also the piece of red flannel she had bought to make herself a new nightgown, which had turned out to be half a yard too short.

Next morning, however, when she was up at the well, she saw Eyelash Jones again. This time he had the apple in his hand, and was polishing it on his sleeve and looking at it wistfully.

"Are you sure you couldn't lend me those teeth? Just once?" he pleaded.

"Never! I'm tired of lending things to you foolish fairies," snapped Old Peg. But then she thought to herself, "Whoa on, wait a bit, my beauty! This could turn out to your advantage, if you bargain with the scallywag." And, aloud, she said: "All right, as a special favour, and because it *is* a nice apple and I hate to see a nice apple go to waste, I will lend you my teeth. But only if you will grant me two things."

The little man's eyes narrowed, for mortals should never make demands of the fairies. "Hmmm," he said. "And what might they be?"

"One," said Old Peg, thinking of the huge tree-trunk that needed splitting, "is that you must promise that the first thing I put my hand on when I get back to my garden breaks. The other," she said, thinking of the red flannel that needed to be longer to make a decent nightgown, "is that you promise that the first thing I put my hand on when I get inside my cottage is made half a yard longer."

Eyelash Jones considered all this for a moment, then he smiled and agreed. Old Peg fished her spare pair of teeth out of her pocket and left him to enjoy his apple. Then she hurried back to her cottage, laughing and congratulating herself on having bargained with a fairy to her own advantage: which people said you could never do.

But people were right.

As Old Peg stretched out her hand to touch the big tree-trunk she slipped on a pebble and nearly twisted her ankle. Bending down, she put her hand on her ankle to rub it—the ankle BROKE, and she fell on her nose! Dragging herself into the cottage, Old Peg rubbed ruefully at her bruised nose. No sooner had she done so than—the nose shot out HALF A YARD!

Luckily for her, Eyelash Jones was not hard-hearted and re-stored nose and ankle to their right condition as soon as he had finished eating his apple. As for Old Peg, she had learned her lesson. The fairies could have anything they asked for, and wel-come, and she would ask for nothing in return. Though, as a matter of fact, they never asked her for her teeth again.

⤸ William Winter ⤷

William Winter was the seventh son of a seventh son and therefore a magician-detective by name, trade and nature. He had studied the grey art of magical detection while still a boy by reading the eight hundred and eighty-eight dusty books in the secret libraries of Toledo, and now he was a man he always had eagle's meat for supper so that he kept clear wits and eyes to practise his skill.

One stormy evening—it was just after the famous case when he recovered the Crown Jewels from the Extraordinary Walking Dustbin of the Utopian Ambassador—he was eating his daily ration of eagle's meat at a corner table in a London restaurant, when four hell-eyed Chinese came in and sat themselves down beside him without a word. William Winter spread some more meat on his mustard and gave no sign that he had noticed them, but before long he sneaked a look in his cup and muttered a magic word (Aldebaran!) so that he could see the thoughts of these strangers swimming in the bottom among the tea-leaves. And he saw that they were robbers, who intended to murder him during the night, and steal his money.

"You tell me please what you do—staring in cup," said one of the Chinese politely, leaning forward and catching the great detective by the wrist.

"Nothing," said William Winter. "Nothing at all."

The Chinese smiled. "You number one liar? You hide something there—in cha cup. Permit me scrutinize, please?"

William Winter pushed cup and saucer towards him across the table. The robber snatched them up and examined both closely.

"Satisfied?" asked William Winter.

"Has dissolved perhaps?" muttered the man, poking about in the tea with his fingers.

"Perhaps," said William Winter. "But if it's conjuring tricks you want, just look at this, my friends." He cupped his hands together in the middle of the table, half-stood up and, bending over, blew between his thumbs three times. "Seratiel, Schaltiel, Chadakiel."

"What is?" snarled another of the robbers, curious in spite of himself.

"There, gentlemen," said William Winter. He opened his hands and sank back in his chair.

The four Chinese gasped. Through a quickly widening crack in the centre of the table a bloodstained finger was fast appearing, pushing up through the wood.

"Look at that!" said William Winter, and then, chuckling, he added, "Yes, look at it all night, until the constable comes."

And that is just what those robbers did, sitting fixed in their chairs all night, staring at the finger, which occasionally beckoned them or waggled in playful reproof. They could not speak, but each of them glared at his companions with one wild imploring eye (the other eye could not leave the finger). The spell was broken only when the constable arrested them, and then the finger, with a final wave, disappeared down through the table and the crack closed and healed so that there was not the slightest mark spoiling the grain of the wood. The constable rubbed his eyes and got down on his hands and knees to search for the finger on the floor, but of course it was not to be found. As for the four Chinese, they were so stiff from being frozen in the one position all night that they had to be carried off to the cells in sitting positions.

William Winter was not really content with successes like this—which he considered small. He was forever looking for a case in which he would have to pit his wits against someone as crafty and cunning as himself.

Then one day a commercial traveller came to the great detective's office and told him of an hotel where people were always being robbed, and no one could tell how. This man had himself stayed at the hotel, which was called The Cat's Arms. When he went to bed he had bolted his door. In the morning the door was still bolted. But all his money had gone, and his trousers too!

William Winter was intrigued. Disguising himself as a commercial traveller, he entered the hotel the next evening and asked for a night's lodging. The Cat's Arms was kept by two sisters. They were both very beautiful, with long black hair and eyes as bright as coals. While the magician-detective was eating his supper (for once, he did not ask for eagle's meat, not wishing to arouse suspicion) the sisters sat by the fire and entertained him. The elder one played the harp while the younger one sang. Her voice was like no other voice that he had ever heard—soft, dark and humming, very sleepy and satisfied, almost, he thought, wiping his plate clean with a crisp crust as he watched her in the corner, fire-shadows chasing across her face and hair, almost like a cat's purring.

William Winter retired to bed early, making a great show of yawning and saying what a long day he had had on the road, how much he was looking forward to a good night's sleep in a comfortable bed, and so on. Before he went upstairs he asked one special favour of the two sisters.

"Certainly," purred the younger one. "What is it?"

The great detective pretended to be nervous and embarrassed. "I hardly like to tell you," he said, "but the fact is—I'm scared of the dark. Silly, isn't it? Especially for a commercial traveller. You can imagine how the other fellows laugh at me!"

"Scared of the dark," purred the older sister. ("So! They both do it!" thought William Winter excitedly, but keeping his face screwed up in a mask of embarrassment.) "Well, what can we do about that, my dear?"

"Perhaps," he suggested, "I might have a big bundle of candles? Then I could keep a light burning all night."

The sisters fetched candles from a cupboard for him and William Winter went up to bed, still yawning. The two women stood in the hallway, silent and staring. Looking down at them to call a last sleepy good-night he thought that they looked just like two cats watching a canary in a cage, biding their time. . . .

As soon as the great detective was safely in his room he stopped yawning and sighing and pretending to be tired, and set about making arrangements for what he thought might well be a busy night. First of all he lit four candles and placed one in each corner, so that the whole room could easily be seen. Then he took off his clothes and heaped them carelessly on the floor, but within easy reach of his bed. In the bed, under the quilt, he hid a short sword that he had concealed in his commercial traveller's attaché case.

Then he bolted the door, climbed noisily into bed, and began snoring as loudly as he could.

He had not long to wait. Soon he heard a most peculiar noise, a scratching, coming from the direction of the chimney. He opened one eye very slightly and saw a cat emerge from the empty fireplace. A few seconds later another cat came out to join the first. The cats crept round the room on cautious paws. Then they began to romp and play, snatching at the bedclothes, chasing each other round the bed. William Winter lay still as a stone, breathing deeply.

At last the cats began to creep towards his clothes. They played about with his shirt for a while. The great detective watched, still pretending to be fast asleep. The cats finished amusing themselves with the shirt and turned their attention to the trousers. But now they were not playing. He saw the smaller cat stretching out her right paw, then putting it into the back-pocket where he kept his wallet.

William Winter jumped out of bed, sword in hand, and struck at the cat's paw! The cat howled and let the wallet go. Both cats raced to the fireplace and disappeared up the chimney before he could stop them.

The great magician-detective was pleased with his night's work. He did not expect the cats back—but, just in case, he put the wallet under his pillow. Then he blew out all the candles and really went to sleep.

Next morning only one of the sisters—the elder—appeared at breakfast time. William Winter asked where the young one was.

"Ill," said the woman briefly, glaring at him over a plate of kippers and a glass of milk.

"I'm sorry to hear that," said William Winter, and proceeded to eat a hearty meal.

After breakfast he got his maps and samples together and told the woman that he must be on his way. "But first of all," he said. "I really must say good-bye to your charming sister. She purr—I mean, she sang so beautifully last night. I shall never forget it as long as I live."

The woman tried all kinds of excuses, but the great detective would not take no for an answer. At last he was shown into the kitchen, where the younger sister sat in a big rocking-chair, gazing wistfully at a kettle on the hob. A gay tartan rug was drawn up to her waist.

"I'm so sorry to hear that you're not feeling yourself this morning," said William Winter. "Perhaps it's the weather?"

"The weather?" muttered the elder sister crossly. "What's the weather to do with it?"

"Well," said William Winter, "it's raining cats and dogs."

The younger sister went red in the face, but did not speak. The older one arched her back, set her face in a hard look and protested that she could not understand this commercial traveller who was afraid of the dark and spoke in riddles.

"No?" laughed William Winter. "Oh well, it's not important. I must be on my way, and no cat-napping here at this time of day with you fine tabb—I mean, ladies. Good-bye." And he held out his hand to the sister who sat by the fire. After a moment's hesitation she withdrew her left hand from under the rug and made to take his.

"Oh no no, my pretty puss," said the great detective, smiling. "I'm not going to shake your left paw—I mean, hand, I beg your pardon. I've never shaken a left hand in my life, and I'm not going to start with yours, white and elegant though it is." And he drew her right hand from the rug.

It was tightly bound with bandages!

"As I suspected," said William Winter, patting her hand gently. "The mystery is solved."

And so it was. You see, the two sisters were witches, and at night they changed themselves into cats—as witches can—and robbed innocent commercial travellers who slept at their hotel. In William Winter, the great magician-detective, however, they had met their match.

"In future," he advised them, "it would be better if you gave up your cat-tricks altogether." And, taking a pin, he seized the older woman's hand and pricked it slightly so that a drop of blood appeared. "There," he said, "now I've drawn blood from both of you, and you won't be able to do any more witch-mischief. Good-day, ladies! William Winter, magician-detective, always at your service! Oh, and—now that you're both, so to speak, retired—please don't hesitate to send for me if you have any trouble with the mice!"

❧ The Lady of the Lake ❧

I

The first time Gwyn saw her his mouth was full of bread and cheese. He had been watching the soft shadows of fish flicker to and fro between sun and clouds in the lake where the sky had fallen, when suddenly he heard singing.

Looking up, Gwyn was astonished to see a Lady walking across the water as though it were a street paved with sunlight. He had never seen anything so lovely. The Lady was tall and walked proudly; her eyes were the colour of the midsummer night; her cheeks were red, her forehead white, her hair long and golden. She sang all the while a song whose words Gwyn could not catch.

Gazing, Gwyn knew that he loved her; and, without thinking,

wanting to offer her some gift as a sign of his love, he held out his hands full of bread and cheese. The Lady stopped singing, brushed back her hair using the smooth surface of the lake as a mirror, and then came slowly towards him over the water. When she was near enough to see what he held in his outstretched hands, she raised her eyebrows, shook her head, and called:

"Boy, boy of the hard-baked bread:
It is not easy to catch me."

Then she sank into the shining water, and disappeared from his sight.

Gwyn went home with a heavy heart full of love for the Lady and told his mother what he had seen. He rather wondered if his mother would believe him—for he was an idle lad and his head was always full of dreams—but for some reason she did not doubt his story.

"Tomorrow when you go to the lake take some unbaked bread, some dough," was all she said. "Perhaps the Lady may like that better."

The next day, before dawn, Gwyn was already waiting impatiently by the side of the lake with the unbaked bread in his hands. The sun rose and melted the mist on the waters. All morning Gwyn watched and waited. Once he thought he saw the Lady's golden hair streaming just below the surface, beyond the jagged green shadow of the reeds—but it was only sunlight gilding the helter-skelter ripples sent skittering by the breeze. Noon came and went.

By late afternoon Gwyn's eyes ached with staring so intently at the bright water, and his heart ached that the Lady had not come.

He was just about to throw the dough angrily into the lake when he saw the water opening like a flower, and the Lady appeared again, ankle-deep in a whirlpool of light.

Gwyn caught his breath, and forgot all the pretty speeches he had prepared. Stretching out his hands, dumbly, he offered her the unbaked dough. The Lady refused the gift with a shake of her head, as she had before, and called:

> *"Boy, boy, of the unbaked bread:*
> *I will not take you."*

So saying, she vanished into the lake again, but before she sank out of sight she smiled such a sweet and sad and tender smile that Gwyn's heart almost burst with love for her. He walked home kicking at pebbles, but then he remembered that smile. "Perhaps next time I can find the gift to win her," he thought to himself.

When he got home he told his mother all that had happened.

"Well," said she, "since the Lady has refused your hard-baked bread and your unbaked bread, it's easy to tell what she wants."

"Is it?" said Gwyn, who did not think it was easy at all.

"Of course. She wants bread that is neither too hard nor too soft, but both together."

"Eh?" said Gwyn. "I don't understand."

"Ninny!" cried his mother. "The Lady wants half-baked bread! Tomorrow you must try your luck with bread that is half-baked. Now if you go and chop some sticks I will make some specially for you in the oven."

That night Gwyn did not sleep a wink. His head—usually so cobwebbed with dreams—was full of nothing but bright pictures of the lovely Lady of the Lake, and the way she had smiled at him. Long before dawn he had snatched up the half-baked bread and run to the lakeside with it. Day broke, the cocks crowing ghostly from a far-away mountain farm, while he peered out eagerly over the water. But the sun soon hid itself behind black clouds, and it began to rain. Gwyn hardly noticed it. Morning wore wetly to afternoon, and afternoon to evening. Still he stood, gazing out over the darkening water dimpled with rain. As night fell and the first few stars began to prick out in the sky Gwyn suddenly became conscious of the soaking wet shirt sticking to his back and the big drops of water streaming down his cheeks. Some of them tasted like tears. He turned brokenly and was about to plod his squelching way home when he heard the lowing of cows behind him—out in the lake!

Gwyn spun round. Cattle, as black as the gathering night, were walking on the top of the water. Gwyn whistled softly. He realized that these could be no ordinary cows—it must be a magic herd. He was sure now that the Lady would soon appear. He smoothed his wet hair and wiped his face as well as he could with his dripping handkerchief. Hardly had he done this when the Lady emerged from the lake, calling softly to the cattle, humming to herself in the dusk. Gwyn was beside himself with love, but it was difficult to see where land ended and water began, and when he rushed forward to meet her, half-baked bread in his hands, he fell—splash!—into the lake.

Gwyn would surely have drowned, for the lake was deep even at the edges, but the Lady caught his arms and drew him up to stand beside her. Smiling, she took his gift of bread and ate it; then allowed him to lead her to the bank. Even in the twilight her beauty dazzled Gwyn; he could only stare and stare at her. As he stared he noticed that the sandal on her right foot was tied in an odd way. The Lady kept smiling at him, so graciously that at last he found his tongue and said, "Lady, I love you more than all the world. Will you be my wife?"

At first, the Lady shook her head. But her eyes and lips still smiled at him, so Gwyn pleaded and pleaded and at last she gave her promise that she would marry him. "But only," she added, "on one condition."

"Anything," cried Gwyn fervently.

"I will marry you," said the Lady, "and I will live under your roof until you have struck me three times without cause. When you strike the third blow without cause I will leave you for ever."

"Lady," protested Gwyn, "I would rather cut off my right hand than strike you. I will never, never——"

He broke off in dismay, for the Lady had suddenly turned her back on him. Running swiftly across the grass, she dived back into the lake. Gwyn burst into tears. He was about to throw himself after her, among the stars riding in the black water, when he heard a shout——

"Stop!"

He looked over his shoulder and saw, on the shore of the lake a little to his left in the direction of the moon, an old man with hair as white as snow. He wore no crown but Gwyn was sure from the way he held his head that the old man was a king. Standing on either side of the old man was the Lady of the Lake!

Gwyn rubbed his eyes. He could not believe what he saw. He walked slowly towards the group, trembling with fear.

The old man spoke kindly. "Mortal, you have asked to marry one of my daughters. I will give my consent and blessing—but only on one condition."

"Anything you s-say," stammered Gwyn.

The old man pointed first to the maiden on his left, then to the one on his right. "You must recognize which of my daughters it is that you love."

Gwyn scratched his neck. He looked first at the maiden on the left. Surely this was his love: her hair so gold, her head so high? But when he looked at the maiden on the right his heart filled with doubt. The two were so alike in every respect that he could not see the slightest difference between them. He thought of closing his eyes and choosing blindly—but the prospect of losing for ever the one who had promised to be his wife, if he chose the wrong one, was too much to bear. He was about to give up the task as impossible when one of the two maidens moved very slightly and quietly, shifting her right foot forward in the dark grass.

Gwyn glanced at the old man, but he did not seem to have noticed his daughter's movement. Gwyn had noticed, however. He had recognized in a flash the strange way the sandal was tied on her right foot. This was his Lady of the Lake—the one who had accepted his half-baked bread. He stepped forward and took her boldly by the hand.

The old man nodded. "You have chosen well," he said. "Be kind and faithful to her and I will give her as a dowry as many sheep, goats, cows, pigs, and horses as she can count in one breath. But—remember!—if you dare strike my daughter three blows without cause, she must return to me."

Gwyn danced for joy, and again protested that he would sooner cut off his hand than do such a thing. The old man merely smiled. Turning to his daughter he asked her to count the number of sheep she wished to have.

She began to count, in fives. "Onetwothreefourfive onetwothreefourfive onetwothreefourfive onetwothreefourfive. . . ." She counted as many fives as she could in one breath. When she stopped, blue in the face, as many sheep as she had managed to count came trotting and baaing in single file, as sheep do, out of the lake.

Then the old man asked her to count all the cows she could. "Onetwothreefourfive onetwothreefourfive onetwothreefourfive onetwothreefourfive. . . ."

Again she counted as many fives as she could in one deep breath. As soon as she stopped as many cows as she had counted came wading out of the lake—black cows, brindled cows, spotted cows, and white cows—lowing and swishing their tails, as cows do.

In exactly the same way she counted as many goats, pigs and horses as she could until the water-meadows were full of animals. Then the kingly old man and his other daughter walked into the water and vanished.

2

The Lady of the Lake and Gwyn were married. All the bells rang and everyone was happy, especially the bride and groom. They lived on the farm together with Gwyn's mother. Everything went well for them. Gwyn worked hard to make his dreams come true and found that he had more than his share of luck and success. Before long, three fine sons were born to them.

One hot summer's day, when their eldest son was seven years old, there was a wedding in a nearby town. The Lady of the Lake and Gwyn had been invited and they set out to walk across the meadows to town, but the sun shone fiercely and soon the Lady stopped in a field where some horses were grazing, sat down under the shade of an oak, began fanning herself with a dock-leaf and declared that it was too far for her to walk and, anyway, she would rather not go.

"We must go," protested Gwyn. "But if you don't want to walk you can ride on one of these horses. I'll go back to the house for saddle and bridle. Will you catch a horse while I'm gone?"

"I will," said the Lady. "While you're about it, bring me my gloves. I left them on the table."

Gwyn ran back to the farm and fetched saddle, bridle and gloves. When he returned, panting, mopping his brow, he found to his surprise that the Lady was sitting in the shade, fanning herself languidly. She had not stirred from the spot where he had left her.

Gwyn stared at her for a moment. She said nothing, looking up at him with a smile almost of pity on her lips. He jerked his thumb towards the horses. She neither spoke nor moved.

Leaning down, Gwyn flicked her playfully on the cheek with the gloves. "Go! Go!" he said.

The Lady sighed. "That is the first blow without a cause," she said.

Gwyn was bitterly ashamed of himself. He had almost for-
gotten the condition. "Still," he thought, "it will be all right: I
will never strike her again."

Seven years passed and then one cold winter's day they were
both invited to a christening. At the party afterwards, gathered
round a blazing log fire, all the guests were laughing and singing
when suddenly the Lady, bending over the cradle to kiss the child,
screamed and burst into tears.

Tapping her brusquely on the shoulder, Gwyn demanded to
know why she wept.

"I weep," she said, "because this poor innocent child is weak
and frail and will have no joy of the world. Suffering and pain
will fill all its brief days on earth, and soon it must die. And I
weep also," she added, "because, husband, you have struck me the
second blow without cause."

Gwyn's heart missed a beat for fear. He swore to himself and
her that he would never strike her again. He knew that the next
blow, the third, would mean the end of their life together, and he
could not bear the thought of the Lady leaving him.

"Never, never again," he promised.

The Lady smiled through her tears and said nothing.

Not long after, when spring came, the poor child whose
christening they had attended, which had always been frail and
ill, just as the Lady had foretold, died, just as the Lady had
foretold. Gwyn and the Lady went to the funeral. There, amid all
the tears and mourning, the Lady suddenly tossed back her golden
hair and began laughing merrily.

"Stop her!" cried the child's father. "She's mad!"

The Lady laughed the louder. Gwyn himself was so ashamed

of her high spirits that he shook her and cried out, "Hush! Hush, woman! Why do you laugh?"

"I laugh," the Lady replied, "because the poor child is at last happy and free from all pain." She brushed his hands from her shoulders as if they had been no more than flies. "And I laugh also," she said, "because the third and last blow has been struck. Farewell, husband!"

She turned and ran from him. Gwyn tried to follow, but found his feet were heavy as millstones. He just could not move from the spot. He pleaded and shouted, but his wife did not look back.

When the Lady arrived back at the farm she went into the fields and called to her cattle: "Onetwothreefourfive onetwothreefourfive onetwothreefourfive onetwothreefourfive. . . .

> "My brindled cow, my much-freckled,
> My spotted cow, my white-speckled,
> Home, cows, home!
> My old white-face, my mottled cow,
> My bull, my grey one, home, all, now!
> And you, my little coal-black calves
> Hung on the hook in dripping halves,
> Come you also home, now, whole!
> Home, cows, home!"

And all the cattle came running to their mistress: the brindled, the freckled, the spotted, the speckled, the old white-face, the mottled, the bull and the grey heifer—even the little coal-black calves, that had been killed and hung up on the hook in halves, became whole again, gave three kicks, and galloped after her.

When she called her sheep, her goats, her pigs and her horses, they came running too. The Lady mounted one of the horses—her favourite, the white stallion—and led them all out of the farm. As she passed one of the fields she saw that there were four oxen ploughing in it. To these she called:

> *"My four grey oxen*
> *Pulling a mortal plough,*
> *Come you also with us:*
> *Home, all, now!"*

The oxen came running, dragging the heavy plough behind them. The ploughboy stood as if turned to stone.

Away went the Lady. She was leading her animals towards the lake. When they reached it she led them all into the water, still riding proudly on her white horse, and they all disappeared beneath the surface, back to where they had come from. The only trace left that they had ever existed was the wild furrow made by the plough which the oxen dragged behind them into the lake. Men say that on moonlit nights this furrow may still be seen; and that when the wind is high across the lake you may hear the Lady weeping for her lost love and for the three blows he struck her without cause.

But some say the sound is more like laughing.

⋘ Cadwaladr's Goat ⋙

Cadwaladr had a goat called Jenny. She was strong and willing, sure-footed and quick-witted. Cadwaladr was very proud of her.

Now Jenny was generally as good as gold, and so gentle you could have caught her with a cobweb, but one fine April evening some mischief got into her head and she would not let Cadwaladr come near her. Round and round the field she ran. Cadwaladr, being on the plumpish side, waddled along behind her, puzzled, making what he hoped were goat-soothing noises. Jenny could not have cared for the sound of these, for she ran faster and faster, her legs twinkling, her head tossing, until with a hop, a skip, and a jump that would have made a kangaroo jealous, she sailed up and over the five-barred gate, disappearing down the road which led to the mountain.

"Hey! Come back!" shouted Cadwaladr, hopefully. But she didn't.

Cadwaladr clambered over the gate and trundled down the road after her. He turned a corner and there was Jenny, standing meek and quiet, half in a telephone box, chewing the telephone directory, like any ordinary goat. But there was a devilish glint in her eyes. She let Cadwaladr come right up to her—then backed out of the box sharply, spun round, butted him, and trotted off again, hooves going clitter clatter. To make matters worse, she kept to the wrong side of the road.

Poor Cadwaladr! He scrambled to his feet and set off in hot pursuit. Through the village, twice round the church, over the railway bridge, under the outstretched arms of the policeman, ran Jenny. And through the village, twice round the church, over the railway bridge, and slap! bang! right into the arms of the policeman ran Cadwaladr.

"Now then, what's all——"

"Sorry no time to say sorry," gasped Cadwaladr. "Lend me your bike, quick! It's my goat!"

"Here, not so fast, that vehicle happens to be the property of the Queen's Constabulary. I could put in an application on your behalf, Form 39 (*a*), the blue one, that is, if you could provide two testimonials as to your——Hey! My bike! Stop, thief!"

"Sorry!" cried Cadwaladr, pedalling away like a plump whirlwind.

"Help! Police!" shouted the constable, blowing his whistle, and

then, remembering that he *was* the police, he put the whistle back in his pocket, took out his notebook, and began scribbling a detailed report (in duplicate) for his superiors.

Cadwaladr, meanwhile, was trying to cycle up the mountain in bottom gear. But the policeman's bicycle was not designed for such exertions, and neither was Cadwaladr. In any case, Jenny soon tired of the road and took to the steep tracks winding in and out between the rocks, so Cadwaladr had no choice but to tumble off the bicycle and continue the chase on foot. By this time, I need hardly add, he was in a thoroughly disagreeable temper.

Jenny did not bother to run very fast. She just kept on trotting up the mountain always a little beyond Cadwaladr's reach. Once or twice she deliberately let him get near enough to lay hands on her back—then she would wriggle and dart off, leaving him to stumble and fall flat on his face. At last she led him right to the brink of a high precipice.

Cadwaladr, out of breath and patience, snatched up a big stone. "You've led me a fine dance, haven't you then?" he shouted. "Well, here's your reward!" And he threw the stone at her with all his might.

The stone hit the poor goat on the nose. She tottered on the edge of the precipice and then fell, bleating, down, down, down. . . .

Cadwaladr suddenly came to his senses and realized the terrible thing he had done. He scrambled back down the path as quickly as he could, tears burning his eyes, and made his way over the rocks to where the goat lay.

Jenny looked up at him sadly. Then she began to lick his hands with her rough tongue. Cadwaladr was so upset by this that he burst into loud sobs. "Forgive me!" he begged. Squatting down on the ground he took the goat's head gently in the crook of his arm, scratching her ears as he knew she liked.

Imagine his surprise when he found soft golden hair like silk beneath his fingertips. The ugly old goat had changed into a beautiful young girl!

The girl smiled up at Cadwaladr. Her eyes were like stars. "My prince, my captain, my own true love," she murmured, "at last I've found you. And how handsome you are!"

Cadwaladr almost swallowed his Adam's apple. No one had ever called him handsome before—not even his mother. "Do you really think so?" he said foolishly, and blushed.

"As handsome as the morning," said the girl. "And when you blush, that's just what it's like—the sun coming up over the lovely dark forests of your moustaches."

"Oh gosh, oh golly," said Cadwaladr. And he blushed some more.

But when he tried to kiss the beautiful girl she turned her head aside and slipped from his arms, rising gracefully to her feet. "Not here, my dearest," she said. "Come with me."

Cadwaladr gave her his hand and the girl led him back up the steep mountain track, talking gently and sweetly all the while. Cadwaladr did not really hear a word she said. He was enchanted by the music of her voice, like a harp played idly by the summer wind, and as he guessed she was saying how handsome, strong, kind, loving, intelligent, he was, or things like that, he did not care about the details. He drew himself up to his full height, which was not much, and strutted like a portly peacock. At one point he did have an uncomfortable idea that the girl's hand did not feel like a hand at all. It was—in fact—well—he hated to say it of such a lovely girl—but it was just a little like a *hoof!* But that was impossible. Besides, when he looked at it he noticed that not only was the hand a hand, but that it was whiter than snow and as fragile and slender as any leaf.

The girl led Cadwaladr higher and higher up the mountain. At last they stood on the very top. Night had fallen and the moon shone brightly in a star-smutched sky. Cadwaladr gazed at the moon and was just going to turn and say something to the girl about it—something sentimental and appropriate—when he realized that the girl was no longer there. He spun round. Behind him, blocking the path that led down the mountain, was a flock of black goats. Their terrible ghostly bleating filled the air.

"Help!" whispered Cadwaladr, then, "Help! HELP!" as loud as he could. But there was no one to hear him; only the moon. Then the largest goat of all—one that bleated as wildly and plaintively as all the rest put together—charged at him, head down, and sent him toppling, spinning, and twisting into empty air, just as he had sent poor Jenny.

Down, down, down went Cadwaladr, the moon all round him, in his eyes and ears, only the moon was bleating and sometimes it was a goat and sometimes a lovely girl and then the moon again, but always bleating, and Cadwaladr must surely have been dashed to death on the rocks below—just where poor Jenny had fallen—if the moon had not taken pity on him and caught him in her arms. At least, that was how it seemed to the dazed Cadwaladr, when he found himself staring the moon right in the face, held and wrapped in the branches of a tree that grew straight out from the sheer face of the mountainside, some way above the sharp teeth of the rocks.

And it was there that the policeman (with his bicycle handcuffed to his wrist so that no one should steal it again) found Cadwaladr in the morning, and with a rope-ladder helped him down safely to firm ground.

Neither the policeman nor anyone else ever believed Cadwaladr's account of what had happened, though they did wonder

how else he could have got himself tangled by his braces in a tree half-way down the side of the mountain. But even though they didn't believe him they could not help noticing how kind and considerate he was to his goats and other animals, from that day on—never hurrying or worrying them, and never, never chasing them up the mountain or throwing stones at them. And the more thoughtful people wondered if there might not be some truth or meaning in Cadwaladr's extraordinary story, after all.

✍ Left Eye, Right Eye ✍

I

An old midwife and her husband once went to Caernarvon to hire a servant-maid at the Allhallows Fair. The custom in those days was for the young men and women who wished to be hired to stand at a certain spot, and when the old couple reached it they at once noticed a girl with hair as red as fire, standing a little apart from the others. The midwife went up to her and asked if she wanted a job. "If it pleases you, madam," said the girl politely. She told them that her name was Eilian and that she was nineteen. A few days later she came to take up her new appointment.

At that time—all this took place, as you might guess, many years ago—it was customary for the womenfolk to do the spinning after supper during the long winter months. The first night she did the spinning Eilian began to weep.

"Why, what's the matter, child?" asked the old woman.

"It's the light," complained Eilian. "It's the lamp hurting my eyes."

"I suppose next you'll be asking us to buy a new one especially for you?" snapped the old man sarcastically, for there was nothing he hated more than a lot of talking while he smoked his evening pipe.

"Oh, no, sir," said Eilian, "I'm sure such a thought never crossed my mind." She ran to the window and peered out through the frost-ferns, then she turned back to the puzzled couple, cheeks glowing. "The moon is shining so rich and bright! Now if I could just take my spinning-wheel down to the meadow I'm sure I could work very well."

Her mistress looked at her sharply. "Are you mad, girl? Spinning outdoors, at this time of night!"

Eilian said nothing, but spread out her hands imploringly.

"Let her go," muttered the old man, puffing at his pipe and reaching for a piece of coal with the tongs. "If she doesn't catch her death of cold she might even do a bit of spinning to keep warm. Heaven knows she'll never do any in here, moaning about a perfectly good light and what else."

Eilian tossed back her red hair, smiled, curtsied, took up her spinning-wheel, and skipped out of the cottage.

The clock ticked, the cat purred on the old man's lap, the old lady got on with her darning. After a while she looked up and said, "Do you think I ought to go and see if she's all right? It's cold enough to turn a body to ice out there."

"Leave her be," advised her husband. "It's only some flighty notion. She'll be back in a minute and only too pleased with the old lamp, I'll warrant."

But Eilian did not come back, and when the hands of the clock both pointed to twelve the old man, who had fallen asleep in his comfortable chair, was suddenly awakened by his wife shaking him and whispering excitedly, "Ssssh! Come quick! You won't believe your eyes when you see what I've just seen!"

Grumbling, half of him still in a dream about a vegetable marrow as big as the Houses of Parliament, the old man allowed her to push him to the window. Looking out, he came wide-awake in a moment. "My whiskers!" he cried. "It's the Fair Family!"

And so it was—the Fair Family, or little people, or fairies as some call them. They were dancing and singing in the frosty, moonlit meadow. And in the middle of the gay green company sat Eilian, the servant-maid, her spinning-wheel turning so fast that sparks seemed to fly from it and stars get caught in it, her red hair tumbled about her shoulders, her face glowing with delight.

The couple dared not tell the girl what they had seen, but they treated her with great respect and care from that time on. Every night when there was a fair white moon she would take her spinning-wheel down into the meadow, and on these occasions an enormous amount of work was done. She never seemed to feel the cold and even went out in crisp deep snow to spin among the Fair Family. The midwife and her husband were well pleased, if a little frightened, to have such an industrious maid-servant.

One spring evening, however, just about sheep-shearing time, Eilian went out as usual with her wheel to the meadow, but did

not come back. She did not come back the next night, nor the next. The old couple found her wheel, with her work piled neatly beside it, but they were sad to have lost Eilian. "She has gone with the fairies," said the old woman, and her husband, sucking thoughtfully at his pipe, agreed that this was probably what had happened..

2

Some months after Eilian's disappearance, on a night of fitful moonlight and drizzle falling through thin mist, there came a clatter of horse's hooves outside the cottage and then a fist banged on the door.

The old man opened it, the poker concealed in his right hand behind his leg, for the hour was late and they were not expecting any visitors.

A stranger stood on the step, his face in the shadows.

"Sir," he said, "I believe your good lady is a midwife. Would you ask her to come with me? It's my wife. Please be quick."

The midwife put on her cape and bonnet and got up behind the stranger on his horse. He rode away wildly through the moonlight, as fast as a swallow, up hill and down dale, through bramble and bush and briar, covering miles of darkness before the poor woman had time even to say Oh! At last he drew rein before a deep cave. Dismounting, the stranger took the old woman's arm. He led her into the cave and then through a door at the far end of it and into a chamber where his wife lay in bed. It was quite the finest place the old woman had ever seen in her life: thick carpets on the floor, tapestries on the walls, and the bed like a galleon of the night, with silken pillowcases and velvet curtains and blankets made of ermine.

In an hour the midwife's work was done, and the lady had been delivered of a bonny baby boy. As the old woman was dressing it in its tiny nightgown and shawl before the fire in the enormous log-filled grate, the stranger came up to her with a bottle of ointment in his hand.

"Would you please rub a little of this on the child's eyes?" he said. "But take care that you do not touch your own eyes with it, or I'll not be responsible for the consequences."

The old woman did as she was asked, being careful not to let any of the ointment go near her own eyes. But, as she was putting the bottle away, her left eye began to itch and without thinking she put the finger to it that she had used for anointing the baby's eyes. Immediately, the whole scene was changed—but only to that eye, for the curious thing was that the midwife now found two rooms before her. With her right eye she saw everything as fine and luxurious as it had seemed to be, but with her left eye she saw a damp, dripping, uncomfortable cave, with a miserable fire flickering in one corner, and the poor mother lying not in a richly-brocaded bed but huddled on a bundle of rushes and withered ferns, with stones all round her. And she saw that the woman was none other than her former maid-servant: Eilian.

She said nothing, not even when with her left eye she noticed little men and women hurrying in and out with dainty food for Eilian, their every movement as light as the morning breeze; but when morning came, and she was packing her bag ready to depart, she leant close over the bed and whispered, "You've many friends now, eh, Eilian?"

The girl started and stared at her. "Yes, I have," she replied. "But how do you know? And how do you know me?"

Then the old woman explained that she had accidentally applied some of the baby's ointment to her left eye.

"Well, just take care that my husband doesn't find out what you've done," advised Eilian. And she told the midwife her story. How she had been helped with her spinning by the fairies, on condition that she married one of them. "I thought I could outwit them," she said, with a wry smile, "and never really intended to fulfil my part of the bargain. I always used to take a twig of rowan with me into the meadow, for no fairy dare cross or touch the rowan, and I thought that that way they could never carry me off. But the day we helped shear Bower's sheep I was so exhausted that I forgot to take the twig with me. And here I am!"

"But you're happy, aren't you, Eilian?"

"Indeed I am. For it's what you see with your left eye that is the real world I live in now, and though it's hard enough it's no grief to me. The right eye is all illusion."

Some time after, the old woman—who had been taken home by the stranger, on horseback, as she had come, and given a purseful of gold for her services—happened to be late in getting to market.

"I reckon the fairies must be here today," joked the greengrocer. "I've had six apples stolen already, and hark at the noise!"

And the fairies *were* there. The old woman could see them with her left eye, swarming about amongst the stalls. Noticing Eilian's husband standing close by and nodding to her, she stepped up to him and said, "Fine morning. And how is Eilian?"

"Oh, she's very well," replied the fairy.

"And the baby?"

"Coming along fine," said the fairy. "But with what eye can you see me?"

"With this one," said the old woman, pointing.

The fairy snatched up a bulrush and pulled out her left eye before she could move or shout. From that day forth the old woman's right eye had to do the work of two, and she saw only the world that Eilian had told her was illusion.

❧ The Boy Who
Taught the Fairies Tears ❧

I

A long time ago, just after the days when there were chocolate
giants and gingerbread palaces and it always rained lemonade, a
boy called Tommy Tacket lived in Babylon Valley over the hills.
When he was twelve years old he was still not much taller than
the kitchen table, and his mother, despairing that he would ever
be much use about the farm, sent him to a monastery to learn his
letters, there being no other schools in those days. Tommy was
not happy among the monks. He liked his ball better than any
book and was in every way a bad pupil. Besides, the monk who
was his special teacher had little patience and he beat the poor boy.
Tommy Tacket determined to escape if he could.

One evening when the monks were at their prayers Tommy crept through the cloisters and climbed over the high wall which shut the monastery off from the outside world. He took a deep breath of clean air and walked for a while on his hands, enjoying the feel of the wild free grass between his fingers, his heart as high and happy as the proud clouds drifting over. Then he was suddenly scared by the cruel clanging of a bell behind him, back beyond the wall, in the monastery, and he ran and ran, not looking over his shoulder for fear the monks were chasing after him. At last, exhausted, he came to a river and sank down on his knees, refreshing his face with brimming handfuls of cold water. Night was beginning to fall so Tommy looked about for somewhere to hide. He found a splendid place in the hollow riverbank and having made himself a pillow of bracken and dragged the trailing branches of a willow across the entrance so that no one would ever suspect he was hidden there, Tommy fell asleep.

Next morning he woke up cold and stiff and hungry, with the sound of voices ringing in his ears. Tommy lay very still. After a while the voices seemed to be coming from farther away so he dared to peep out between the branches of the willow. He saw three monks walking in the hayfield on the other side of the river. Their robes were kilted up to avoid the dew and they all carried white sticks, poking about and switching irritably at the tall grasses. Tommy was very frightened at first, being sure they would find him. But when one of the monks—the same fat, red-faced teacher who had succeeded in knocking any love of learning out of the boy—looked straight at the part of the bank where he lay hidden and then walked on without a word, Tommy realized that they would never find him if he stayed where he

was. He even began to enjoy himself by pulling faces at the
monks' backs as they strode away from him across the field.
When they had all three disappeared from sight he lay back down
in the hollow bank and wondered what he was going to do
now.

A rumbling in his belly reminded Tommy of the worst of his
problems: food. He did not dare go out and look for a cottage
where he might beg a crust of bread or a bowl of milk, for the
monks would certainly have spread the news of his escape
throughout the surrounding countryside, and he knew no one he
could trust. Tommy grew hungrier and hungrier as the sun took
its time across the sky. When darkness fell he slid out cautiously
and picked a few berries, but these did little to satisfy his hunger
and he had trouble in getting to sleep. He dreamed all night of the
monk with the cane and woke up sobbing.

"Hey, Spikk, look at this," said a voice at his elbow. "Here's a
mortal with his eyes full of water. Have you ever seen such a
thing?"

Tommy Tacket scrambled into a sitting position. Brushing the
tears from his eyes with his sleeve he peered into the gloom and
made out the figures of two men, no bigger than himself, standing
just inside the entrance.

"How do you do that magic?" asked one of the little men
politely.

Tommy was ashamed that they had seen him crying. "It's no
magic," he said. "I'm hungry and unhappy, that's what."

"What's unhappy?" asked the other little man. "We know
what hungry is. It's when there's no gingerade."

Tommy frowned. "You mean lemonade."

"No, I don't," said the little man. "When I say gingerade I mean gingerade. Gingerade's gingerade and lemon beer's lemon beer. Everyone knows that."

Tommy shrugged his shoulders. "Well, that would be thirsty, anyway," he said. "Hungry is when there's no cakes, or meat, or bread."

"What's cakes?" demanded the first little man.

"What's meat?" demanded his companion.

"What's bread?" they both demanded together.

"You don't know cakes!" cried Tommy, smacking his lips. "Why, cakes are—cakes are like—like—oooh, Great Jumping Eclairs, I'm so hungry!" And he drummed on his empty, aching belly with his fists.

The little men looked at each other with serious faces.

"I think we might invite him," said the first.

"If the King didn't mind," said the second.

"Do you suppose he would be angry?"

"Well, I don't fancy the prospect of toadstool-drill, do you?"

"No, or circle-bashing!"

"But he seems a nice boy—for a mortal, that is. Not too many lies yet, you'll notice."

"But they'll come later."

"Still, he is hungry."

"Very hungry."

"Very, very, VERY hungry!" shouted Tommy, rolling his eyes.

The little men laughed. Tommy thought he had never heard such a happy sound: it was like a holiday in the head. "I'll tell you whatsoever," said the first little man, "we'll take you with us if you'll teach us that magic with the eyes. How to spin them round and round, that is."

"And how to do that lovely unhappy," piped the second little man, "with the water in the eyes and all."

Tommy smiled. "I'll teach you that if you like," he said, "but you'd really be better without it. Anyway, where are you going to take me? Who is this King of yours?"

"Why, *the* King, of course," explained the first little man.

"Come along! Stir your stumps! Look sharp! Watch your step!
Buck up!" He turned to his companion. "You must admit, Spann,
I handled those mortal idiots rather well."

"Idioms, Spikk."

"Eh?"

"Oh, never mind. By the march: quick! right!"

And each of them took hold of one of Tommy's hands and
began to tug him towards the back of the hole in the bank.

"Wait a bit," he protested. "Where are we going? This is just a
hole—we can't go back any farther because—oh!"

Tommy Tacket caught his breath in astonishment. The two
little men had pressed with their tiny thumbs at two blue stones
embedded in the wall of the hole and part of it now swung
inwards like a door. It *was* a door, concealed so cunningly that
Tommy had not noticed it in all the time he had been in his hiding-
place! Beyond the door was an underground passage, just big
enough to allow him to scramble along it. Tommy had never been
so pleased that he was small. He followed the little men down into
the darkness, heart thumping.

2

The tunnel was not long. Soon they came out into a strange and
beautiful country. Tommy had never known anything like it.
The rivers purred like sleepy cats, the meadows were filled with
jewels instead of flowers, the woods echoed with the singing of
invisible birds whose notes hung on the air like rainbows. Every-
where there was a perpetual twilight. Looking up, Tommy saw

that this was because the sky was not blue but obscured with thick clouds of a curious earth-colour. The sun was nowhere to be seen.

"It never shines here," explained the first little man casually, noticing the boy's puzzlement.

"We don't need it," added the other.

"Nor the moon?" asked Tommy.

They shook their heads.

"Not even the stars?"

"No, not even the stars. Now you teach us that rolling magic——"

"And the nice unhappy magic, with the water."

So they all three walked along through the strange country, Tommy Tacket teaching the two little men how to roll their eyes. At first they just went cross-eyed and staggered about holding each other up; but they soon mastered the trick and were rolling their big eyes round and round like mad millwheels. Tommy was glad, however, when he found that try as they might his new friends could not learn to cry. They made him tell them all the most dismal and depressing stories he had ever heard; but then they only shook their heads sadly and looked embarrassed. They tried rubbing their eyes, and blinking for minutes on end—but their gaze remained innocent and undazzled, and they just could not squeeze out a single drop of the slightest shadow of a tear.

"Never mind," said Tommy, seeing their disappointment. "Perhaps we can find an onion somewhere. Peeling that would make you cry!"

But the little men had never heard of onions.

3

At last they came to a palace built entirely of precious stones, and Tommy Tacket was brought before the King and introduced to him in the presence of the court. The King was only about two feet tall, but plump as a pumpkin. He had rosy cheeks and long white hair, and he sat on a throne cut from a single diamond as big as a horse's head. On either side of him stood lords in red and ladies in green. Not one of them was tall enough to come much above Tommy's shoulder.

"You are welcome, Tacket Esquire," said the King, when he had listened to the report of Tommy's two companions and the boy's own stammered story. "You may dwell amongst us for as long as you wish, so long as you take nothing from our Kingdom back to Upper Earth. While you are here with us it would please me greatly if you would play with my son, and perhaps educate him in the weird ways of mortals like yourself." He clapped his hands, and a boy of about Tommy's own age stepped out shyly from behind the throne.

"Hullo," he said. "My name is Prince Pennroyal."

Tommy bowed awkwardly.

"No need for that," whispered the boy. "And, if we are to be friends, you can call me Pen. All right?"

"All right," said Tommy, grinning. And they shook hands.

"Now," said Pen, when they had excused themselves from the court and stood outside its doors of beaten gold, "what would you like to do first? Go and watch the hare-horses? Or play enchanted marbles? Or count up to infinity-and-one with the golden balls?

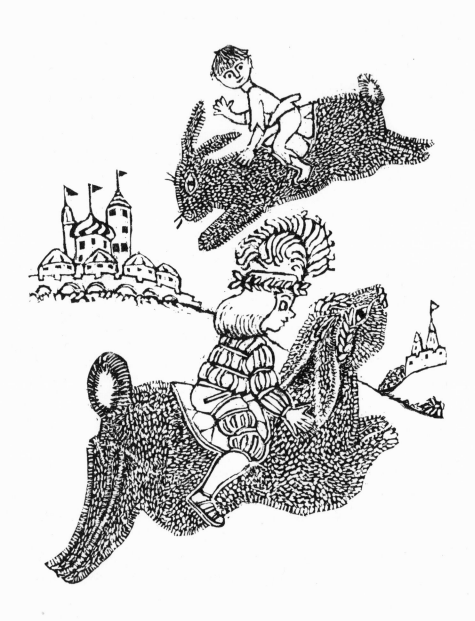

Or shall we learn some Innocence?"

Tommy, not understanding what any of this signified, rolled his eyes. "What I'd love more than anything in this world or any other," he said, "is a good square meal."

"How do you eat squares?" asked Pen. "And how do you do that rolling magic? I'll tell you whatsoever: you come along to the kitchens with me and we'll have a nice dish of milk and saffron mess."

"*What?*" shrieked Tommy. "That sounds awful!"

"It's lovely, really," said Pen. "Besides, it's all we ever eat down here, so you'd better get used to it. Come on, and you can show me how to do that eye-rolling. I saw Spikk and Spann doing it in court as they brought you in, so it can't be all that hard."

Tommy Tacket was very happy in this strange Kingdom and soon became acquainted with all its ways. Its inhabitants were all of the smallest stature, but not stunted, dwarfish or misshapen as you might suppose. Their complexions were fair, and their flaxen hair long and thick, curling down to their shoulders. They rode about on giant hares just like horses, without bit or bridle, but with saddles the size of pocket-handkerchiefs, fashioned from lily-pads. They ate neither flesh nor fish (nor cakes! Tommy noted with dismay), but lived on gingerade, lemon beer, vanilla ice-cream, and milk flavoured and made up into a kind of porridge with saffron. (This was not so bad once you got used to it.) They never took an oath; they never told a lie; they detested nothing so much as falsehood. Whenever Spikk or Spann or any other members of the special brigade that performed what they called Upper Earth Duty—that is, keeping a watch on the activities of the world above—returned to the palace, they were always full of scorn for the ambitions and follies and treacheries and trickeries of men. The little people seemed to worship no gods; but they loved Truth above all things.

After a week or a month or a year (there being no sun and no clocks it was difficult to tell how time passed) Tommy began to feel homesick, and he begged Pen to use his influence with the King to obtain permission for him to go back up and visit his mother for a while. Pen was doubtful. "How do I know you won't want to stay up there once you're home again?" he said. But Tommy pined and pleaded so miserably, and gave so many promises that he would return, that in the end Pen gave in and spoke to his father about it.

The King granted permission and, accompanied by Spikk and Spann, Tommy was allowed to make his way through the tunnel and visit his mother as often as he wished, protected by invisibility until he was safely over the threshold of her cottage. Mrs. Tacket was overjoyed to see him again, for she had long supposed him dead or lost for ever. She questioned the boy closely about his new home, and at last he told her everything, after swearing her to secrecy.

4

Now one day when Tommy was visiting his mother he happened to mention the big golden balls which Pen used to count with.

"Gold, you say?" Mrs. Tacket grinned as she huffed on her tea, for she was a greedy woman and a plan was taking sly shape in her mind. "I don't believe you."

"Mother, I don't tell lies," protested Tommy. "The little men have taught me otherwise."

"The little men! The little men! That's all I ever hear: little men this and little men that. But *I*'ve never seen them and for all I know they don't exist outside your foolish head," sneered his mother. "You say there are two of them out there now, hiding in the branches of the old sycamore, waiting to take you back down

to your precious silly Kingdom—but I never see anything do I? I suppose I'm not good enough for such fine treats? Now if you were to bring one of those gold balls for me to have a look at next time. . . ."

"But that's stealing," said Tommy, "and, besides, the King has often told me I must never take anything from his land and bring it up here. I don't want to offend him."

"Sooner offend me then, would you?" whined the old woman. "You think more of that fat little fairy upstart than you do of your own mother, is that it?" And she began to weep and wail. "I don't know what I've done to deserve such a son, who won't do a thing for his own flesh and blood but is for ever gallivanting off, up hill and down dale, with a lot of heathen, good-for-nothing——"

"Stop it!" shouted Tommy. "I'll bring one of the balls next time I come to see you, if that's what you want. I promise it."

His mother pinched his cheek. "There's my good boy. I always said your heart was in the right place."

"But you can't keep the ball," added Tommy, wretchedly. "I'll have to take it back. I'm only fetching it so that you'll know I'm telling the truth about Pen, and the King, and all the little men, and their magic land down there."

"Of course, of course," cooed his mother soothingly. "You just get one of those gold balls to show me, that's all, and I'll never doubt another word you say, my duck."

Well, a few days later, when Pen had gone out for a ride on his favourite hare, Tommy tiptoed down to the royal schoolroom and took one of the golden balls from the counting-box. Then he walked out of the palace as calmly as he could with the ball concealed under his coat, and set off in the direction of the tunnel to Upper Earth. There was no one about and he was confident that he had not been seen. The little people trusted him now, and he could move about quite freely without arousing suspicion. All the same, when he drew near the underground passage Tommy began to run. He scrambled through it, clutching the ball to his chest. As he clambered out of the hole in the bank he fancied he heard small, quick footsteps pattering in the darkness behind him and he began to run like the wind, head down, for home. When he reached the sycamore that stood not far from his mother's cottage he sneaked a glance over his shoulder and saw Spikk and Spann, their usually cheerful faces blotched red with rage, chasing over the meadows after him. For a moment Tommy thought of turning back and offering the ball to his friends—but then he heard Mrs. Tacket calling from the kitchen-window, "Quick, you blockhead! Run! Run for your life!"

And he ran.

Tommy reached the cottage only a few yards in front of his pursuers. His mother pushed open the door for him and he rushed in, stumbled on the threshold, and fell headlong, the golden ball jumping out of his arms and rolling heavily across the floor.

Mrs. Tacket bent eagerly to scoop it up, but even as she did so Spikk and Spann leaped over the boy where he lay sprawling and snatched it from her thin and reaching fingers. Then they turned and ran from the house, spitting on Tommy as they trampled over him.

"Theep chief!" snarled Spikk.

"Yes," panted Spann. "And cheap thief, too!"

His mother was weeping and cursing, but Tommy ignored her.

As soon as he had his breath again he ran back to the river and searched up and down it for the hole in the hollow bank, the underground tunnel that led to fairyland. But he could not find it. He called after Spikk and Spann and Pen himself, begging forgiveness, and he scratched and dug and tore at the soil with his fingernails, his heart and eyes overflowing with harsh grief and shame. But he could find nothing. The door to the land of delight was closed in his face for ever.

After many weeks of useless searching Tommy Tacket returned to the monastery. Eventually, he killed his love for fairyland by becoming a monk himself. Or so men said. As for Tommy, or Friar Eliodorus as he was now called, he said little, and it was hard to persuade him to speak at all of the happy days he had enjoyed among the little men. And when he did tell the story he always left out the most terrible part of all, the thing that he did not dare remember too well for fear it would break his heart. You see, when Spikk and Spann had spat on him with such disgust and despair in their eyes, Tommy Tacket had noticed something else glittering there too. And he did not want to be known as the boy who had taught the fairies tears.

❦ The Magician's Revenge ❧

A thirsty magician—for magic is thirsty work—once went into a tavern and asked for a glass of beer and a bite of bread and cheese. The beer was flat and warm, which good beer should not be; and the bread and cheese tasted as though it had come crawling from the nearest mouse-trap. The magician did not complain, for that was not his way. But when he asked how much he must pay and the landlord said tenpence—sixpence for the beer, and fourpence for the bread and cheese—he grew very angry inside, for he considered this an outrageous sum for such poor stuff, all this being in the days when beer and bread were cheap. Still, the magician handed over ten pennies without a word. But before he went out he took a piece of paper from the crown of his tall black hat, scribbled something on it, and hid it in a toby jug on the mantelpiece.

Now the landlord happened to be a lazy man, and his wife was not much better. Soon after the magician had gone they both began yawning like kittens and shuffled off to bed, leaving their barmaid to look after things. Their heads had hardly touched the pillow when they heard a terrible shouting and banging downstairs. The maid was dancing on the bar and screeching at the top of her voice:

> *"Six and four are ten:*
> *Add it up again!"*

Angrily, the landlord, dressed in his long white nightshirt and his red nightcap with the black tassel, padded to the top of the stairs and called down, "Oi! Jemima! What's the matter?"

Jemima kept on dancing.

> *"Six and four are ten:*
> *Add it up again!"*

she shrieked back, by way of an answer.

"The baggage! She's gone bonkers," muttered the landlord to himself. He thumped downstairs, hoisting up his nightshirt to the knees, so that he should not trip and tumble in the hem of it. He was a fat, important-looking man, and always moved slowly about his business so that people should know what was what and who was who. As soon as he set foot in the bar, however, he hitched up his nightshirt even higher, gave a hop, snatched the maid's hands in his own, and joined in her crazy dance up and down the bar-counter, bellowing:

> *"Six and four are ten:*
> *Add it up again!"*

Upstairs, his wife was sitting bolt-upright in bed, patting her curlers. When she heard her husband's fruity voice joining in the idiotic chant she did not know what to think or do. She tried banging on the floor with the chamberpot. She tried screaming. She tried putting her head under the pillow (this only upset her curlers). At last she could stand it no more. Leaping out of bed she rushed to the top of the stairs and shouted to them to be quiet, for what would the neighbours say?

Back came the answer, from two voices:

> *"Six and four are ten:*
> *Add it up again!"*

The landlady slid fiercely down the banisters (she always did this—she was thin as a matchstick and it saved time). When she saw her husband in his nightshirt prancing about with the maid and yelling:

> *"Six and four are ten:*
> *Add it up again!"*

she quite lost her temper. Snatching up a broom, she bounded into the bar, intending to knock them both over the head. Instead, she found herself waving the broom like a baton and tapping her irritable toes, and—yes!—there was her own scratchy voice, joining the others in the silly chorus:

"Six and four are ten:
Add it up again!"

With three voices bellowing away the noise was deafening. Soon all the neighbours—the carpenter and his wife, the baker and his four daughters, the butcher and his two sons, and the schoolmistress—came running in to see what was the matter. Before long the room was packed with men and women, some in nightshirts, some in big boots, some in their Sunday best, all skipping about hand-in-hand and calling, in piccolo voices, trombone voices, bugle voices, and one or two voices like war drums:

"Six and four are ten:
Add it up again!"

Only one person, Jack, the cobbler's son, did not get caught in the dance. This was because Jack was a shy boy and he always peeped in at the window before entering a house. When he saw the whole village dancing in the bar-room he thought at first that they were all drunk. Then he noticed that his father was dancing with the schoolmistress. He knew that *she* could not be drunk, and at the same time he remembered seeing the magician coming out of the tavern earlier that evening, when he had been playing with his ball against the high wall. "It's that magician who's at the bottom of this!" he said to himself, nose pressed against the window.

"Six and four are ten:
Add it up again!"

answered the whole village, so loudly that the pane of glass shivered and shook and almost splintered with the noise.

Jack ran and ran and ran. He caught up with the magician just as that gentleman was about to disappear for the night.

"Sir," he cried breathlessly, "you must break your spell!"

The magician smiled. "They are all dancing?"

"Every one!"

"And they are all shouting:

'Six and four are ten:
Add it up again!' ?"

demanded the magician.

"Yes, sir," said Jack.

The magician chuckled, then fumbled in his cloak and consulted a watch as big as a saucer. "Very well," he said, "I daresay by the time you get back they will have learned their lesson in that village. They shouldn't overcharge customers, you know—especially not magicians. But you're a bright lad—I saw you catching that ball on the tricky spin, very fine—you just nip back now and when you get to the tavern march straight in with your fingers crossed and look in the toby jug on the mantelpiece. You'll find a piece of paper with some magic on it. Whatever you do: *don't read it*. Burn it, and then they'll stop their row. Oh, yes," he added, "and before I disappear, here's a magic ball for you. You'll find it always comes back to your hands, no matter where or how hard you throw it, so long as you say this magic word."

And he told Jack the word (which of course cannot be printed here or it would burn the page).

Then Jack thanked the magician, put the ball in his pocket, and raced back to the village. He went into the tavern with his fingers crossed, pushed his way through the dancers, found the paper and thrust it on the fire without reading what was written on it.

At once the dancing and the shouting stopped. All the dancers fell down, panting and exhausted. No one was more exhausted than the fat landlord, who had been made to look ridiculous, which he could not bear. However, when Jack had explained to the company exactly what had happened and what he had done (without mentioning the magic ball) the landlord decided to put a good face on it. "Free drinks and fresh bread and cheese on the house," he declared—and everyone had some, even the schoolmistress (not beer, but a sip of dry sherry and a nibble of cheesestraw).

And from that day on, the tavern sold beer and bread and cheese at reasonable prices, especially to magicians. And, whatever you bought there, it was a funny thing—as everyone remarked—but the landlord never let the bill come to tenpence.

᥍ Above the Wind,
With the Wind,
or Below the Wind? ᥲ

As soon as Gwen saw it she knew it was a fairy dog. It had a body as white as snow and ears as red as blood; it lay close to the ground, pink tongue lolling. Gwen knelt and stroked the dog and it licked her hands, all buttery from the churn. She could feel its tiny heart beating, pit-a-pat, pit-a-pat.

"Poor little morsel, what frightened you then?" she muttered. To tell the truth, Gwen was frightened herself because she remembered what had happened to her friend Beryl Bean when *she* found a fairy dog. Beryl had no time to be kind to animals and she had not treated the strange creature well, refusing it water and milk and a soft cushion and not finding a juicy bone for it from her larder.

Next day a cross-looking little man in a red cap had stopped Beryl as she was calling the cows home from pasture. The little man spoke gruffly, biting his words off. "Well, girl, which is it to be: above the wind, with the wind, or below the wind?"

Realizing that this was no ordinary mortal who stood before her, Beryl curtsied. "Please, your honour, I don't understand."

"You will soon," said the fairy. "I'm asking you to choose which way you want to go: above the wind, with the wind, or below the wind?"

Now, if Beryl had been a sensible sort of girl, with her wits about her, she would have said "with the wind," which would have meant a pleasant enough spin through the air at a reasonable height, once round the church spire, say, and back in time for supper. "Above the wind," as you might guess, is a terrible journey, up, up, up, till you'd think your head would bump on one of the lower stars: not at all nice, especially if you don't like heights. Beryl didn't, not of any sort, so she answered: "If your kind honour pleases, I'd be well satisfied with below the wind."

The little man chuckled grimly and stamped three times, snapping his fingers in her face. Immediately Beryl was seized by invisible hands and whirled along the ground, through bramble and briar and blackberry bush, her nose rubbed thoroughly in the cow-turds, her hair washed horribly in the thick green scum on the standing pools, until her dress was torn off her back and she found herself face-down in the ditch outside her home, a chicken perched on her head, and her body black and blue all over!

These things raced through Gwen's mind as she wrapped the fairy dog warmly in her apron and carried it, safe and soft, all the way home. She gave it sweet milk in a saucer, a fatty bone to gnaw at, and made up a comfortable bed for it in the pantry on big cushions stuffed with the finest lambs' wool. The fairy dog looked grateful, but you never knew. Gwen did not sleep easily that night. "If he asks *me*," she muttered, over and over, "I must say 'with the wind. . . .' I must say 'with the wind. . . .'"

First thing in the morning there came a sharp knock at the farmhouse door. When Gwen opened it she saw the little man she had heard of. His face was bad-tempered, and he wore a red cap, just as Beryl Bean had described him.

"G-good morning," said Gwen. "C-can I——"

"My dog," snapped the little man. "Where is he? Don't tell me any lies or it will be the worse for you."

"Oh dear! oh dear!" cried Gwen, tears in her eyes. "With the wind please, sir. I'm very sorry to have offended. With the wind——"

Just then the fairy dog came bounding past her. It jumped straight into the little man's arms and began licking his face affectionately. As for the little man, he bent his head so that the dog could whisper in his ear. He listened carefully for a few seconds, then his face changed. All the thunder went out of it. Gwen thought that she had never seen such a big grin in all her life. It seemed to stretch right across his face and round the corners too.

"I know now that you have treated my dog well," said the little man, raising his red cap, "and I thank you for it. He's always chasing rabbits and getting lost and it's such a bother worrying around after mortals to see whether they've been kind or unkind to him."

"Well, it's been no bother to me to be nice to him," said Gwen. "He's a lovely dog. No trouble at all. So—if you don't mind, sir—can I please go *with the wind?*"

The stranger beamed. "I don't think there's any call for that, on this occasion," he said. "But I will ask one question, as thanks for your kindness. Think very carefully now before you answer. The

question is this: which would you rather have, a clean cowyard or
a dirty cowyard?"

Gwen was just about to say "a clean cowyard of course,"
thinking that the fairy was going to clean it for her, when she
noticed the dog. It was shaking its head vigorously, the red ears
flopping, and if ever a dog spoke without saying a word this one
did: and what it said was "dirty."

"Please, sir," said Gwen, "a dirty cowyard."

The little man nodded. "You have chosen rightly, because no
one can have a clean cowyard unless they have very, very few
cows. As it is—I think that when you go to call the cows in for
their morning milking in a minute you'll find you have two cows
for every one you had last night! Good morning, and thank you!"